TEA PARTY TODAY

To Marcia, Betty, Elaine, and Diana—my Tuesday morning teamates.
—E. S.

For Ruth and Jim Johnson, with love.
—K. D.

TEA PARTY TODAY

Poems to Sip and Savor

by Eileen Spinelli

Illustrated by Karen Dugan

Wordsong/Boyds Mills Press

Introduction

I received my first tea set—blue-and-white willowware—on my fourth Christmas.

My father, clever with tools, built me a table and chairs. My mother, creative with a needle, sewed me a brightly colored tablecloth.

I remember feeling so excited on the occasion of my first tea party that my hand shook as I poured tap water into my doll's tiny teacup.

When I was six, my best friend, Gladys, and I had front porch tea parties. My folks provided apple juice "tea," and her mother supplied oatmeal cookies.

There were cozy tea times at my Aunt Rose's brick row house in South Philadelphia. Tea was served in an antique Chinese teapot with a bamboo handle. There were warm squares of gingerbread dolloped with applesauce. In the background, music poured from an old mahogany player piano.

"Tea" at my grandparents' took place on a plaid blanket in the side yard. There, amid purple and yellow iris (my grandmother called them "flags") we sipped fresh-squeezed orange juice and ate figs, dates, and walnuts.

My wish for the readers of this book is that someday you will have warm tea-time memories of your own.

Contents

Market Day

The beekeeper's daughter
Is charming and fair
With clover all woven
Through braids in her hair.
She travels through villages
Hamlets and farms
With a basket of honey
Hung on her arm,
Singing:
"Bless the blossom and
Bless the bee.
Honey for sale
For cakes and tea.
Honey for sale
For cakes and tea."

Teatime tip: Honey comes in many flavors: clover, orange-blossom, buckwheat,

raspberry, and more. Check your nearest market.

Shopping for Tea

Which tea shall I buy today?
English breakfast? Earl Grey?
Ginger? Sassafras or spiced?
Rosehip, orange, lemon-iced?
Apple, peppermint, or peach?
Oh, just give me one of each.

Teatime tip: Plan a tea-tasting party. Try to have at least five different kinds of tea. Take a vote on the favorite.

Invitation

Behind the King's roses
The Queen is a bee
And honey's for children
To stir in their tea
And biscuits are cookies
And jam is a treat
That butterflies taste
On their flutter-by feet.
The kettle is cozied
By lemony sun.
Requesting your presence—
Come join in the fun.

Teatime tip: Don't invite someone to tea over the telephone. Write your invitations by hand on nice notepaper. Create your own notepaper, perhaps in the shape of a teakettle or on a small paper doily. Send it in the mail or deliver it in person.

Getting Ready

I gather tulips, daffodils.
Tea party today.

I dust the table, mop up spills.
Tea party today.

I rinse each saucer, every cup.
I line the spoons and napkins up.

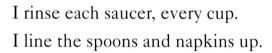

Tea party today.

I wash my face and comb my hair.
I choose the clothes I want to wear.
I put some cookies on a plate,
Then hang the sign on my front gate:
TEA PARTY TODAY!

Teatime tip: Have everything ready—including your smile—five minutes before teatime. Somebody always arrives early.

Discovery

The kettle is boiling
The scones are set out
The company's hungry
And gathered about
And though you seem cozy
And snug, little mouse,
I warn you, Mom's teapot
Is not a safe house.

Teatime tip: Check for mice. Use a flashlight.

12

Kitchen Music

Pots clank.
Glasses clink.
Water gurgles
In the sink.
Beater whips.
Blender whirs.
Clock ticks.
Spoon stirs.
Mug plunks.
Fork pings.
Best of all—
Kettle sings.

Teatime tip: You and your teamates can add to the music. Hum. Whistle. Snap your fingers. Clap your hands. Tap your toes. And how about a sing-along?

Teatime

Teatime, teatime
Here's the tray
Cups and saucers
Pink and gray
Linen napkins
Copper pot—
Come and get it
While it's hot.

Teatime tip:

Start your own cup-and-saucer collection. You'll find bargains at yard sales, flea markets, and thrift shops. All cups and saucers don't have to match.

Teatime Grouch

The cake is too sweet.
My bread is too thick,
And as for this jam—
It makes me sick.
My cup is cracked.
What else is wrong?
The milk's warm
And my tea's too strong.
A storm is brewing
Just ahead—
I knew I should have
Stayed in bed.

Teatime tip: Sometimes the best thing to give a grouch at teatime is a hug.

What's That Racket?

Geese honk
Cows moo
Ducks quack
Doves coo
Snakes hiss
Bears growl
Owls hoot
Wolves howl
Chicks peep
Horses neigh
Lions roar
Donkeys bray
Pigs oink
Dogs bark—
Time for tea
On Noah's ark.

Teatime tip: Invite your friends to "Noah's Tea." Ask them to bring along stuffed animals. Serve animal crackers.

Please

You may put sugar
In your tea
Or milk
Or honey from the bees
You may prefer
A lemon squeeze
Or choose to use
None of these.
Just don't put in
Your fingers
Please!

Teatime tip:

Other things that are fun to add to your tea: a thin slice of orange, a spoonful of preserves, a splash of apple juice, a sprig of mint.

Adventure

I had tea with a dragon
And lunch with a mouse.
I've lived in a seashell
Instead of a house
Once I even went diving
With dolphins and whales
From the deck of a ship with
Sun on her sails.
I danced in the forest,
Flew to the moon,
Soared across town
In a hot-air balloon.
Adventure is never as hard as it looks
You'll find it, like me—
In the pages of books.

Teatime tip: Ask your guests to name a favorite book character with whom they would like to have tea.

Lakeside

The water's blue
And so's the sky
Oh what a lucky
Child am I
To have my tea
In such a place
With sunlight dancing
On my face.

Teatime tip: Think about interesting places other than your dining room where you might have tea. How many different places to have tea can you find in this book?

Seaside

The sun provides us golden light
The surf provides the song
You bring the picnic basket
And a tablecloth along
I bring a book of poetry
To read throughout the day.
The sea gulls bring their appetites
And whisk our crumbs away.

Teatime tip: Teatime and poetry make a splendid pair. Encourage your teapartners to bring a favorite poem with them.

Delicious

The air's a whiff of minty tea
A froth of cream spills from the sea
The sun is golden soup, so hot
The sky, a big, blue porcelain pot
Brown sugar beach is soft and sweet
This day is good enough to eat.

Teatime tip: Recipe for Minty Tea.
Fill a quart pitcher with water. Add six tea bags. Count out ten mint leaves and add to the water. Place pitcher in refrigerator overnight. Serve the next day with sugar or honey to taste. Goes well with shortbread cookies.

Tea For One

A cup of tea
A quiet nook
A cookie and
A picture book
A lump of sugar
On my spoon—
Now that's a
Perfect afternoon.

Teatime tip: Friends away?
Nobody around to ask to tea? Invite yourself!

24

Teddy Bear Tea

When I am feeling lonely,
Out of sorts, or blue,
When there's no one to play with
And nothing much to do,
I pat a pretty mud pie,
Set cups beneath a tree,
And host a backyard party
For teddy bear and me.

Teatime tip: Mud pie manners: *Pretend* to eat mud pies. Do not really eat them. Do not use your parents' good forks, spoons, or pie plates. Wash your hands when you are finished.

Tea Around the World

In Ireland tea is cozy.
In Russia tea is strong.
In China tea is served to guests
And sipped the whole day long.
In Burma tea is pickled.
In Turkey, sold on streets.
In England tea comes on a tray
With sandwiches and sweets.
Japan has rules for formal tea
And one is wear your socks.
Go to Tibet and you would have
To chip your tea from blocks.
Moroccans favor green tea
With mint and sugar, too.
My favorite place in all the world
For tea is home with you.

26

Teatime tip: Plan a tea around another country. Visit the library to learn about the country. Focus on decorations and food. Learn how to say "tea" in different languages.

Summer Twilight

Supper's over
Chores are done
Front porch swims
In setting sun
Rockers beckon
Tea is cold
Children gather
Good as gold
Eight o'clock
The house clocks chime.
Grandpa says:
It's story time.

Teatime tip: Invite grandparents and other older relatives to tea. Ask them to tell stories about when they were children.

Cozy

There's a lot to be said
For a tea tray in bed
On a cold winter night
Lost in moon-dappled light.

When the wind's blowing hard
Through the trees in your yard
I can promise you this—
Tea and blankets are bliss.

Teatime tip: Does a cold winter night make you think of a different beverage? Substitute hot chocolate or spicy apple cider for tea!

Welcome on a Stormy Night

Come in from the rain,
The thunder, the chill,
Come in from the wind
On your face.

Come take off your coat,
Your hat and your boots,
Come sit by my fireplace.

I'll warm you with quilts
And peppermint tea.
We'll talk by
The fire's soft light.

And should the storm last
We'll call up your folks
And tell them
You're spending the night.

Teatime tip: For overnight tea guests, fill a basket with a toothbrush, comb, soap, book, a foil-wrapped chocolate mint, and other items.

Published by Wordsong
Boyds Mills Press, Inc.
A Highlights Company
815 Church Street
Honesdale, Pennsylvania 18431
Printed in Hong Kong

Publisher Cataloging-in-Publication Data
Spinelli, Eileen
Tea party poems : poems for children / by Eileen Spinelli;
illustrated by Karen Dugan. 1st ed.
[32]p. : col. Ill. ; cm.
Summary: An original collection of poems about tea and tea-time,
including recipes and tips.
ISBN 1-56397-662-5
1. Children's parties Juvenile poetry. 2. Children's poetry, American.
[1. Parties Poetry. 2. American poetry.] I. Dugan, Karen, ill. II. Title.
811.54-dc21   1998 AC   CIP
LC Card Number 97-77901

First edition, 1999
Book designed by Tim Gillner
The text of this book is set in Caslon Roman.

10 9 8 7 6 5 4 3 2